Rocky Cave Kids

THE DRAGON STONE

Rocky Cave Kids

THE DRAGON STONE

by **Dian Curtis Regan**

illustrated by **Stacy Curtis**

Marshall Cavendish Children

To Anna and Bo Maldonado

Text copyright © 2011 by Dian Curtis Regan
Illustrations copyright © 2011 by Marshall Cavendish
All rights reserved
Marshall Cavendish Corporation, 99 White Plains Road, Tarrytown, NY 10591
www.marshallcavendish.us/kids

Library of Congress Cataloging-in-Publication Data

Regan, Dian Curtis.
The dragon stone / by Dian Curtis Regan. — 1st ed.
  p. cm. — (Rocky Cave kids)
Summary: Miggy, who lives near Rocky Creek in Triassic Forest with the
rest of her Clan, finds a rare dragon stone that must be kept a secret lest
it lose its magical powers.
ISBN 978-0-7614-5974-3 (hardcover) — ISBN 978-0-7614-6085-5 (ebook)
[1. Cave dwellers—Fiction. 2. Dinosaurs—Fiction. 3. Prehistoric
animals—Fiction. 4. Magic—Fiction.] I. Title.
PZ7.R25854Dr 2011
[Fic]—dc22
2011000036
Editor: Margery Cuyler
Printed in China (E)
First edition
10 9 8 7 6 5 4 3 2 1

CONTENTS

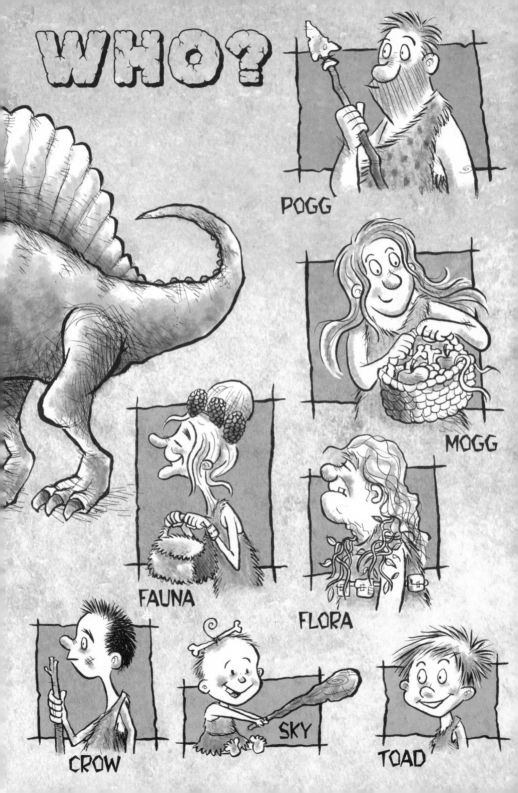

CHAPTER 1

A GOOD SPOT TO SPY

Miggy dropped an armful of sticks onto the ground.

"Thank you," said her mother, Mogg. She tossed a few into the fire pit outside their cave near the banks of Rocky Creek.

Excitement wiggled inside of Miggy like the dancing flames. Summer was drawing to a close. All her friends would be coming back to Triassic Forest before the Clan's annual festival.

During the warm months, her friends moved to cooler climates so their fathers could hunt mammoths.

Not *her* father, Pogg. He made tools to sell. Her mother made baskets and clothing decorated with seeds and shells and bits of bone. Her family did not need to follow the herds.

"Miggy!" came a shout from the grassy

meadow on the other side of the creek.

Miggy squinted into the bright sun to see who was calling. Stone! *He's back from the hunt!* she thought. *Yay!*

"Come on!" Stone hollered.

"Go play," Mogg said. "I'm stringing acorns today and won't need any help until Toad wakes from his nap."

Miggy was only too happy to dash off across the log bridge over the creek. Playing with Stone sounded much more fun than babysitting her little brother.

She hurried along the winding path through the meadow. "Hey, don't run so fast!"

Stone stopped to wait for her at Turtle Rock where the forest began. His dark hair was as long as hers and just as straight.

"Hurry, then," he said. "I don't want to miss it."

"Miss what?"

"Woolly's pogg told him that someone caught sight of a Spinosaurus at the dinosaur pond. Woolly went out this morning to see if he could find it."

Miggy stopped to catch her breath. "Woolly is back in Rocky Creek, too?"

Stone made a goofy face. "If he wasn't, how could he have gone Spin hunting?"

Good point, thought Miggy.

A Spinosaurus was a rare sight in Rocky Creek. Not even her parents had seen one. Catching a glimpse would be as thrilling as finding a nest of wild turkey eggs. *Which,* Miggy added to herself, *are beige with brown spots.*

Her class had learned to identify eggs last spring. A Spin's eggs were not only gigantic, but they were pale lavender, the color of lilacs.

Miggy thought it was amazing that a Spin had wandered into Rocky Creek for the first time in years. As she followed Stone into the forest, she imagined coming face-to-face with the creature around every bend.

If they spotted it, they could claim to be the first to see a Spin. Everyone in the Clan would be in awe. No wonder Woolly had gone looking for it.

Stone left the path and started up a hill that led to a high cliff. Miggy followed, careful not to step too close to the bittersweet vines snaking around tree trunks.

The grannies had warned them not to touch bittersweet because it would make them sleep for three days. Miggy definitely did not want to sleep through the festival.

The grannies, Flora and Fauna, were sisters. They knew things. Miggy figured they knew *everything*.

Up ahead, Stone stopped hiking and turned to face her. He put a finger to his lips. "Let's be quiet so we don't startle the Spin if he's at the pond."

They had come to the end of the wooded path. Above them, huge slabs of flat rocks, the pale color of grass in winter, reached to the edge of Half-Moon Cliff.

The cliff had gotten its name because it curved inward, making the shape of a half-moon. It looked as if a hungry mammoth had taken a bite out of the hill.

Hunching over, Stone moved quietly up the slanted rocks. He used both hands to steady himself. When he reached the cliff, he lay on his stomach and peeked over the edge.

Miggy followed. She was almost too excited to join him. What if a Spin were down there right now, looking back at her?

She peeked. No sign of the Spin.

From their spying spot, Miggy and Stone had a full view of the pond below. Yet they were too high up to be seen by any creature that might think they'd be tasty.

A T. Rex and her baby splashed and played in the water. Two elk grazed along the bank. A wild boar was making its way through the bellflowers near the pond.

But there was no Spinosaurus.

Stone dropped a rock off the cliff and watched it land in a bed of pine needles. "I guess we didn't get here fast enough."

"Maybe he'll come back," Miggy said. "Let's wait."

She felt determined to stay for as long as it took. How could she give up a chance to see a dinosaur she'd only heard about in stories told around the fire pit?

CHAPTER 2

DON'T TELL

The pond below was as round as a hawk's eye. Purple wildflowers and bear grass grew along the bank. Ten paces away, tall pines reached toward the sky.

In the middle of the pond, a giant rock jutted out of the water. As Miggy watched, three crows landed on its flat top.

Since she loved naming things, she decided right then and there to name the rock "Three Crow Island."

Before Miggy could feel too pleased with herself, a flock of chitter birds swooped over the treetops and dove into the pond. Seconds later, they rose up with fish in their beaks.

Miggy hoped the chitter birds wouldn't fly over the cliff and dive at her. The grannies warned not to let a bird pluck your hair and carry it off to its nest. Otherwise, your head would throb each time the bird laid an egg.

Just to be safe, she scooted sideways beneath a jutting ledge to hide from the birds. "Ouch," she said, looking to see what was jabbing her in the side.

Miggy picked up an egg-shaped rock the size of her palm. Jaggedy lines the color of blood berries snaked around the creamy oval.

Her heart soared as high as the chitter birds. *It's a dragon stone!* The jagged lines looked like claw marks left by the mama dragon herself.

For years Miggy and her friends had searched for dragon stones. But they'd never found any. The stones were well hidden in the hills and valleys of Rocky Creek.

If you were lucky enough to find one, the stone would bring you luck and grant your wishes. That is what the grannies had always said.

I found a dragon stone!

All the things Miggy might wish for spun through her mind: A bigger work area for Pogg? He seemed cramped in the dark hollow of the cave where he made tools.

Help for Mogg? With her weaving and cooking; tanning hides for clothes; searching for berries, nuts, and herbs; and taking care of Toad, Mogg could really use some help.

And for me?

Maybe she'd wish for a visit from her fun uncle Flint. He lived with the Mountain Clan, beyond the forest where snowcapped peaks touched the clouds. He was a famous inventor, best known for inventing pockets.

"Guess what?" Miggy said, excited to show her prize to Stone. In a flash, she remembered what *else* the grannies had said about dragon stones: they bring luck *only* if their owners keep them a secret.

"What?" Stone asked.

Oh, feathers. Her excitement drooped like

the tail of a dead squirrel. "Um, nothing," she said.

Stone clicked his tongue as if he wasn't in the mood to be teased. He went back to watching the T. Rex hurry her baby out of the pond.

A small and quick Velociraptor had come to drink. Miggy wondered if the giant T. Rex was afraid of the small raptor.

Taking off her belt pouch, she secretly slipped the dragon stone inside. Now what? Stone would notice the bulging pouch and ask her what she was carrying.

Perhaps she'd better hide the dragon stone for now. When it was time to leave, she'd carry the pouch in her hand so Stone wouldn't notice it.

Miggy slid the pouch beneath a bush on the edge of the cliff. She couldn't wait to take it home and hide it so her curious little brother wouldn't find it. Maybe the best place would be in the dry grass beneath her sleeping mat.

Soon the dragon stone would bring her luck and grant her wishes.

She grinned just thinking about it.

CHAPTER 3

DANGER ON THE PATH

As Miggy and Stone waited, they heard a rustling in the trees behind them.

Something was coming up the hill!

Miggy hunched close to the ground. Fear tickled the back of her neck.

Was it a raccoon?

Or something larger?

With sharp teeth?

Like a . . . a saber-toothed tiger?

Or what if the Spin had decided to climb the cliff?

Uh-oh.

Miggy glanced at Stone. His face was as pale as the rocks. "We're trapped," he whispered.

Staying low, they scuttled around the curve of the cliff to a spot where scraggly bushes grew. The bushes weren't much of a hiding place, but

they were better than nothing.

Miggy picked up a few rocks in case they needed to protect themselves from any wild animal that might spring out of the trees.

That plan had worked after a bear had surprised Miggy when she was with her friends Willow and Twig near Lizard Lake. Maybe it would work a second time.

Miggy thought of her uncle Flint's favorite saying:

> *Lucky once*
> *Danger twice.*
> *Lucky twice.*
> *Paradise.*

As Miggy held her breath and waited to be lucky twice, something burst through the trees at the top of the path and started up the flat rocks straight toward them.

CHAPTER 4

SCARY AND NOT SCARY ANIMALS

It was an animal all right.

Two animals.

Woolly and Twig.

"Phew!" whispered Stone.

Miggy felt as relieved as he did. And she was happy to see that Twig's family was also home from the summer hunt.

She watched her friends climb the steep slope. Woolly was tall. His wild hair looked like a lion's mane. Twig was as skinny as her name and wore her hair chopped short.

"Let's scare them for scaring us," Miggy whispered.

Stone agreed. He took a few of the rocks Miggy had collected and aimed carefully at the sloping cliff.

His three quick throws were perfect, setting

14

off a landslide of pebbles that slid and tumbled toward their friends.

Twig shrieked. She had the best shriek in the Clan. An awesome shriek. Miggy wished *she* could shriek as loud as Twig. Woolly fled down the path and found a fat tree to hide behind. He peeked around the trunk to see what sort of creature might be chasing him.

Miggy thought it funny that Twig stood her ground while Woolly ran away. Twig was brave.

Lifting her chin, Twig sniffed the air like a wolf. Her eyes scanned the top of the cliff until she spotted them.

"I see you!" she hollered.

Miggy waved.

"That was *not* funny," Woolly called. He kicked the tree, acting as if he'd *meant* to run away and wasn't really scared.

Grinning, Stone and Miggy waited for their friends to climb up and join them.

"It was funny to *us*," Stone said, ducking as

Twig gave him a pretend punch.

Woolly nodded in the direction of the pond. "Did you see it?"

"No," Stone replied. "But you did, yes?"

"Noooo," Woolly answered, sounding dis-appointed. "A friend of my pogg's caught a glimpse of its tail as it disappeared into the trees. I want to be the first in the Clan to see it. *All* of it, not just its tail."

Woolly climbed to the very top of the cliff and sat down. The others joined him. "How was everyone's summer?" he asked.

"I caught a snake as thick as a swamp vine and as long as one too," Stone told them. "It took four people to carry it back to our travel-ing tent for supper."

"One night, I saw strange glowing lights stretching from one side of the dark sky to the other," Woolly said.

"I got to swim in a lake so big, giant fish swam along with me," Twig said. "And the

water tasted like salt!"

The stories grew more amazing. Miggy said nothing because nothing exciting ever happened to her.

How could it when she stayed home to help Mogg weave reeds and find seeds? And help Pogg polish axe handles and bury cuttlefish bones to prevent lightning from striking too close to their cave?

These were not the types of stories to tell your friends because it would make them yawn.

But now Miggy *did* have a story to tell. She could hardly sit still. Something amazing *had* happened to her. Finally!

Yet she had to keep the fabulous secret of the dragon stone all to herself or its magic wouldn't work.

Not fair! Miggy thought, letting out a disappointed sigh.

Not fair at all.

CHAPTER 5

A CLOSE CALL

Suddenly, a giant Pterodactyl swooped across the sky and landed on the rock jutting out of the pond below.

"Oh, look!" Miggy said. "He's come to visit Three Crow Island."

"Visit *what*?" Twig asked.

"The island in the middle of the pond," Miggy explained. "I named it."

Woolly scoffed. "Why do you always have to name everything?"

Miggy crossed her arms. "Because it's fun and I'm good at it."

Woolly playfully pitched a pebble at her.

Miggy ducked. "Remember how you wanted to name your baby sister 'Waaaah' because that's the only sound she ever made?"

The others laughed.

"Okay," Woolly said. "You *did* have a better name for her. Sky. Because her eyes matched the color of the . . ." Pausing, he pointed up.

"And your mogg agreed with me," Miggy reminded him.

Woolly shoved his wild hair back from his eyes. "Yes, she did. You win. You're the best at making up names."

Before Miggy had time to enjoy the moment, the ground began to tremble. Slightly at first, then more and more, until the cliff shook and grumbled.

"It's him!" cried Stone.

Twig let out a shriek—but just a tiny one because they hadn't actually seen anything yet.

The water in the pond sloshed against the shore as the rumbling grew.

The group stayed still, waiting for the Spin to step into view.

And they waited.

But the trembling got softer and died away.

"Oh, bear tracks," Woolly muttered. "Spin must have just been passing by."

"Or he's very shy and doesn't want us to see him," Twig added.

Everyone looked so glum, Miggy tried to think of something cheerful to say. "Why don't we give up for now and go see if Willow and Crow have returned to Rocky Creek?"

"Good idea," said Stone.

Miggy started to touch the pouch on her belt to make sure the dragon stone was still inside. Then she remembered: She'd taken off the pouch and hidden it beneath a bush.

Miggy hurried across the rocks to snatch it up. But when she reached the spot on the edge of the cliff where she'd left it, the pouch—with her precious dragon stone inside—was gone.

CHAPTER 6

FOUND AND LOST

Miggy followed the others down the path. She was in a daze. How could her lucky dragon stone have disappeared before she even had a chance to take it home?

Plus, her heart pinched over the thought of losing the beaded pouch Mogg had made for her when she started school four years ago. But the item *inside* the pouch was more precious than polished river rocks.

What had happened to it?

Miggy replayed the past ten minutes in her mind.

Ah, she thought as she remembered the mini-earthquake the invisible Spin had caused. The vibration must have bounced the pouch right off the cliff.

Miggy steered around a clump of bittersweet

vines. She felt so sad she did not even want to catch up with Stone and the others to see what they were talking about.

She ran her hand across the tops of the feather plants as she thought it over. She should not have set her prize so close to the edge of the cliff.

Miggy felt like crying. What if a dinosaur stepped on it? What if someone else found it, and the magic worked for them and not for her?

She wanted to race to the bottom of the hill and circle around to the pond, but the afternoon sun slanted across the treetops. Now was the worst time to go anywhere near the pond since animals came to drink before nightfall.

She'd have to wait.

Twig stopped so Miggy could catch up. "Why are you being so quiet?"

Miggy plucked a leafy branch from a sugarberry bush to shoo away the gnats. "No reason," she said, hoping Twig wouldn't ask any more questions.

If she couldn't tell a soul about *finding* a dragon stone, the last thing she wanted was to tell a friend about *losing* it.

CHAPTER 7

WILLOW AND CROW

At the bottom of the hill, the group headed south. They cut through a grove of buckthorn trees that led into the woods. These woods were as familiar as the inside of their family caves. They'd spent their whole lives exploring this part of the forest.

Coming out of the woods, the group followed Rocky Creek until they came to the place where a fallen oak made a fat bridge across the rushing water.

They crossed the bridge one at a time and entered a grassy meadow with a fishpond in the middle. Permian Park. This is where the festival would take place tomorrow.

Beyond the park, another trail led to the Mastodon Mountains. As the group started up the steep mountain path, Crow came around a bend.

"Hello!" he called, waving a walking stick. "We're back!"

He seemed taller to Miggy. He must have grown over the summer. But his hair still stood straight up like the grass in the park.

As the friends greeted Crow, his sister came down the trail.

"Willow!" Miggy called, waving. "Welcome home!"

Miggy and Twig immediately fussed over Willow's new bone necklace. Since the girls in Rocky Creek usually copied Willow, Miggy figured they would all be wearing bone necklaces by the time snow began to fall.

"Did you learn any new jokes over the summer?" Woolly asked Crow.

"Of course!" he answered. "What would you do if you found a Stegosaurus sleeping in your cave?"

No one answered. They knew better than to guess at Crow's jokes.

"You would look for another place to live."

"Booooo!" said Twig as the others groaned.

The group hiked up the mountain trail until they came to Woolly's cave. His pogg, Old Tanner, greeted them. Old Tanner made musical instruments for the Clan.

Woolly's baby sister, Sky, sat on a leather blanket. She was pounding on a tree stump with a drumstick her father had carved from a branch.

Miggy sat down on the blanket next to Sky. She felt a special connection with the baby she had named.

Old Tanner was getting ready for the festival by stretching hides over hollow logs to make drums. "Take one and try it out," he said to Miggy.

He handed her a drum the same size as Sky's tree stump. She began to beat on the hide with her hands. Sky helped.

Willow sat beside them.

"Here's a rain stick," Woolly said, handing Willow a hollow stick with sunflower seeds inside. When she tilted it one way, then the other, it sounded like falling rain.

Twig joined them with a flute carved from a mammoth's tusk. The boys started to choose instruments as well, but a pheasant wandered across the clearing, and they dashed off to chase it.

Twig fingered notes on the flute while Miggy beat the drum.

Old Tanner gave them pointers.

Willow kept time with the rain stick.

Sky mostly giggled and clapped.

Miggy made up a song to go with the beat:

Summer is coming to an end.
I make music with my friends.

The girls sang the song low. They sang it loud.

They sang it slow, then fast.

They sang it until the boys came back with

the pheasant as a gift for Old Tanner and his family.

When it was time to go home for supper, Miggy glowed with happiness. She loved the changing of seasons when all her friends came home to Rocky Creek.

If only she could ask for their help in the morning. But her secret mission was something she had to do alone: Go to the dinosaur pond and search for her missing dragon stone.

CHAPTER 8

THE SECRET SEARCH

In Miggy's dream, her entire cave was built of creamy dragon stones. Lumpy, oval walls with jaggedy blood berry lines surrounded her.

The dragon stones gave off an eerie glow, lighting the inside of the cave like a basket of fireflies.

Her dream had just circled around to the part where all her wishes were about to come true, when someone jumped on top of her, yanking her awake.

Toad.

"Why are you up so early?" groaned Miggy, making room for him on her sleeping mat.

Instead of answering, he put his head down and promptly fell asleep.

"Fine, you can have my bed."

Getting up, she felt a chill in the air. Time

to start wearing shoes again.

Miggy dressed quietly so she wouldn't wake her family. With luck, she'd collect her missing dragon stone and be home way before it was time to leave for the festival.

She smoothed her sheath and then put on a bracelet strung with walnut shells. Twig and Willow had made walnut-shell jewelry too. Miggy enjoyed the soft rattle the shells made when she moved her arm.

Stepping outside, she smiled at the rising sun and clear sky. Rain wouldn't dare spoil today's celebration.

Miggy climbed onto a flat boulder beneath an apple tree and pulled a leafy branch low enough to pluck two small apples for breakfast. Then she hurried across the log bridge Pogg had built over Rocky Creek.

On the other side, Miggy came to a fork in the road. One path led to the stone archway at the entrance to Rocky Creek. The other led to

Turtle Rock and the forest beyond.

Miggy followed the path toward the forest, chomping on both apples. Across the meadow, the sun was shining on Stone's cave. She wished she could holler at him to wake up and come with her. But she knew she couldn't.

As she passed Turtle Rock, Miggy gave it a pat.

"Guess who gave Turtle Rock its name?" she sang to the mist flowers growing along the path. "Me, me, me!"

The top of the rock *did* look like a turtle sunning himself. After she pointed it out to Pogg, he'd thought it clever of her to notice. He even told Mayor Magnon.

At the next Clan gathering, the mayor declared that the boulder along the pathway would be called Turtle Rock from then on. Remembering that day made Miggy smile.

Deep in the forest, she came to the path leading up to the cliff. But instead of taking it, she made her way along the base of the hill.

As the path curved toward the pond, Miggy tried to be extra quiet. Why had she put on her walnut bracelet? The shells rattled every time she moved her arm.

If only she could remove the bracelet and put it into her belt pouch, but the pouch was just as lost as the dragon stone.

Around the next bend, Miggy spotted the top of Three Crow Island above the trees. That's how she knew she was near the pond.

She stopped and stayed hidden until she was certain no large animals roamed the banks.

Looking up through the trees, Miggy focused on the top of the cliff. Where was the pouch sitting before it fell? *Oh, yes,* she thought, as she remembered. *I'd scooted beneath the ledge so the chitter birds wouldn't dive at me.*

Miggy walked close to the sheer wall of the cliff, following its half-moon curve inward. She kept one eye on the pond in case something large rose from its depths.

A large bird fluttered past, startling her. She watched it swoop toward the water and nab a fish. She hoped the bird did not mistake her for breakfast.

The thought made her laugh. This, in turn, surprised a squirrel that scurried from her path and made her jump again.

Two deer grazed between her and the pond. They did not worry her. Deer usually ran from humans.

Miggy kept glancing at the top of the cliff until she was directly below the spot where the pouch fell.

Beneath her feet, the ground was spongy with soft grass and pine needles. She knew the dragon stone was protected in her pouch. Still, she was glad to see it had a soft place to land.

Miggy bent the tall grass out of the way to start her search. A few rocks looked out of place. Maybe they also fell from the top of the cliff when the Spin caused the earth to quake.

She checked beneath them, just in case. But she did not spot the pouch anywhere.

Keep looking, Miggy told herself.

Would a small animal have lifted the pouch and moved it? Could it have gotten caught in one of the shrubs? Or on the branch of a tree before it even hit the ground?

Miggy pushed through a grove of saplings and stepped into the shallow cave at the base of the cliff.

A nest!

She stepped closer to see better.

There, at her feet, was a nest of gigantic eggs. Pale lavender eggs.

Oh, feathers! These are Spinosaurus eggs!

And there, in the middle of the nest, sat the dragon stone, peeking out from the top of her pouch.

CHAPTER 9

SHOCK AND AWE

As Miggy reached for the dragon stone, two things happened that sent her heart to the stars and back:

Stone came crashing through the trees in a mad dash toward her. A look of shock froze on his face when he saw her.

And just as suddenly, a growling yowl burst from behind him.

Something was chasing Stone!

He leaped for the nearest tree. "Climb!" he shouted.

But Miggy held back.

In a flash, she reached into the Spin's nest, grabbed the dragon stone, and firmly shoved it into the pouch.

Then, instinct took over.

Miggy raced to the tree Stone had chosen.

Holding the pouch with her teeth, she used both hands to pull herself up to the highest sturdy branch.

With one hand, Miggy clutched the pouch. With the other, she held onto the branch. "What happened?" she gasped, out of breath. "Why are you here?"

Stone looked a bit guilty. "I thought if I came to the pond at dawn, I might find the Spin and be the first in the Clan to see it. But instead, I surprised a Velociraptor."

Miggy could tell by his shaky voice he'd had quite a fright. Hooking her feet beneath a branch to steady herself, she quickly fastened the pouch with its treasure onto her belt.

"What have you got in there?" Stone asked.

Before Miggy could think of an answer, the yowling raptor found their hiding spot.

The small, quick creature pawed the trunk of the tree with its tiny arms and claws but could not climb up.

Thank the stars, Miggy said to herself.

The raptor let out a shrill shriek.

"Uh-oh," Stone said. "I think he's calling for help."

Instantly, two more raptors came flying through the forest. They stopped beneath the tree, kicking up dirt.

Silently, Miggy and Stone gazed down at the creatures with their strong legs and large, scaly snouts.

The raptors stared back with beady eyes, as if they were looking at a yummy breakfast.

Yummy breakfast? Miggy thought. *Yummy breakfast equals Stone and me!*

CHAPTER 10

TRAPPED!

"How are we going to get out of here?" Stone asked in a breathy whisper.

Was he thinking the same thing Miggy was thinking?

Storytellers who traveled through Rocky Creek told tales about people taking refuge in trees when chased by raptors. But it didn't mean they were safe.

True, the creatures could not climb up to get them, but they could *outwait* their prey.

And we are their prey, Miggy told herself.

The tales always ended with people either falling out of a tree as they slept, or starving while waiting to be rescued.

Miggy shivered as she remembered tales about travelers finding skeletons in trees.

"We're doomed," Stone said in a quiet voice.

"I didn't tell anyone where I was going. Did you?"

"No."

Miggy figured Stone assumed she'd come to the pond at dawn for the same reason he did—in hopes of catching a glimpse of the Spin.

And, Miggy thought, *the Spin is probabl nearby since its nest is below.*

She nervously scanned the forest surrour ing them. The last thing they needed right n was for the Spin to show up. The long-jaw creature could simply pluck them from the t

Another raptor came crashing out of woods, snapping Miggy's attention back to danger at hand. Now there were four crea watching them.

She looked at Stone. Tears filled his That's exactly how she felt. If only one of had told their parents where they were they could at least expect to be rescued.

They needed to come up with a plan

Oh, wait! She *had* a plan!

Opening the pouch, Miggy slipped her hand inside and wrapped her fingers around the dragon stone.

What words was she supposed to say to make the stone grant her wish?

Suddenly, her hand began to tingle. The dragon stone warmed, almost as if it had come alive for a moment.

"I should have brought my whistle," Stone said. "Someone might be close enough to hear us."

"It's not all your fault," Miggy said, trying to make him feel better. "I didn't think to bring my whistle, either."

The raptors were prancing and gnashing their sharp teeth. Two of them began to pound the trunk of the tree with their powerful tails.

Terrified, Miggy grasped a branch with her free hand. Could the raptors knock the tree down? Or knock them out of the tree?

"Hold on!" Stone cried.

Miggy focused on the dragon stone, squeezing it tight.

Dragon stone, please save us from this danger! she shouted in her mind.

The raptors froze in unison, as if their mothers were calling them from afar. One bounded off through the trees. Then the others fell into line and followed, without looking back at their victims even once. They seemed to have forgotten why they'd gathered beneath the tree in the first place.

"Oh my feathers!" Miggy cried.

"Did you see that?" Stone said, touching her arm. He was shaking. "They aren't going to eat us after all."

Miggy took a deep breath. She couldn't believe it. The dragon stone had honored her wish. It had saved their lives!

She drew her hand out of the pouch. *It really works!*

"Let's get out of here while we have a chance," Stone said.

They climbed down from the tree and dropped to the ground. Heading the opposite direction from the way the raptors had gone, they hurried along the trail at the base of the cliff.

After they'd put a good distance between themselves and the creatures, Stone slowed down to pluck a pear from a low-hanging branch. "I'll bet the Spin isn't even hanging around the pond any longer. I'll bet he's moved on to wherever Spins go for the winter."

Miggy glanced back to make sure they weren't being followed. Should she tell Stone he did not need to think about the Spin leaving? That dino wasn't going anywhere. She'd built a nest! She was planning to stay in Rocky Creek—at least until her babies hatched.

CHAPTER 11

A TINY, FUZZY SPIN

"*There* you are," her mother said when Miggy arrived home. "Where have you been?"

Before Miggy could answer, Mogg continued, "Will you please take your brother on a walk while I finish getting things ready for the festival?"

Miggy longed to tell her mother about the raptor scare at the pond. But, of course, she couldn't. The dragon stone was a secret.

Toad was being Toad, tearing around, getting too close to the fire pit, and climbing into the neatly piled crafts Mogg was planning to take.

"Come on, Toad," Miggy said. "Let's go for a walk." *I'll hide the dragon stone when I return,* she added to herself.

"Me stay," chirped Toad.

"No," she told him. "Mogg has things to do."

Toad began to wail.

Miggy sang him a silly rhyme she'd made up when he was born:

> *Wave bye-bye*
> *to stars in the sky.*
> *The stars go to sleep*
> *as the sun starts to creep,*
> *as chicks start to peep,*
> *and toads start to leap.*

Usually it made Toad stop crying and listen. By the time she got to "toads start to leap," he would start leaping around and giggling.

But this time, it didn't work.

"Toadie, let's go see if the baby bunnies are still in the nest behind Turtle Rock."

Toad stopped sniffling the instant baby bunnies were mentioned.

Miggy hoisted her brother onto her shoulders so they could go faster. She headed north toward the log bridge over Rocky Creek.

As soon as they were a hundred paces away from home, every little noise spooked her. She knew she was reacting to her raptor scare of the morning.

Jangled nerves and all, Miggy carried Toad across the bridge and along the meadow path toward Turtle Rock.

When they arrived, she set Toad on the ground. "Shush now, so we don't scare the bunnies."

Holding hands, the two tiptoed around the boulders. Miggy searched for the nest Mogg had found while picking coriander to rub into the meat Pogg had brought home.

She spotted the nest in a hollow of the boulder, hidden behind tall grass. "Look!" Miggy whispered to Toad. Three babies were in the nest. Even though they were rabbits, they looked very much like tiny brown mice.

Toad looked up at Miggy. "Ig?"

That's what he called her. "Ig." He couldn't say "Miggy" yet.

"Yes?" she answered.

"Names?"

"The bunnies don't have names," she told him.

At that moment, Miggy wanted to name the bunnies in the worst way. But then again, she wanted to name *everything*.

Sighing, she stifled the urge. Toad should get to name them. After all, he had the idea first.

"Would you like to name the bunnies?"

Toad's grin was as bright as the yellow poppies dotting the meadow.

"Fuzzy!" he shouted.

His shout startled the bunnies. They began to tremble.

"Let's name them quieter," Miggy whispered.

"Brownie," Toad whispered back.

"Fuzzy and Brownie," she repeated. "Good names. What about the third one?"

"Mmmmm," Toad said. He picked a tiny

pink flower as he thought about it. "Spinny!"

Miggy laughed. Toad must have overheard the adults talking about the mysterious Spin in Rocky Creek.

"Okay. The bunnies will always be known as Fuzzy, Brownie, and Spinny."

Toad giggled. He held out the pink flower. "Mogg!"

"Is the flower for her? She will love it."

A sharp whistle tickled Miggy's ear.

Pogg.

"Time to go home," Miggy said. "Pogg is whistling for us."

Toad looked very pleased with himself. He hopped toward the path as if he were a bunny.

"Wait for me!"

Miggy ran to catch him. "I will teach you a song. I made it up yesterday at Old Tanner's."

Toad slowed down to listen:

> *Summer is coming to an end.*
> *I make music with my friends.*

He tried to sing along but could only remember some of the words: "Mer come end. Make my friend."

Miggy clapped. "Good job, Toadie. I'll race you home."

He blasted off again. Boy, her brother could run fast.

Miggy let him go since this part of the path was straight. She figured he'd be tired by the time he got to the bridge. She knew he'd wait for her.

As she walked, Miggy adjusted her belt pouch. She liked keeping the dragon stone with her, even though she knew it wasn't a good idea. Sooner or later, someone might catch a glimpse of it and figure it out.

Then what would happen? Would the stone's power fizzle and fade? She did not want to take that chance.

Slipping her hand into the pouch, she felt its smooth roundness. The stone was so powerful!

see her reach into her belt pouch. As her fingers curled around the dragon stone, the familiar tingling and warming began in the curve of her hand.

Miggy closed her eyes. *Dragon stone. Free my brother from this snare.* Then she added, *Please.*

In the time it took Miggy to draw her hand from the pouch and open her eyes, the vine around Toad's ankle fell away.

Toad yanked his leg free and wobbled to his feet.

Miggy could see a reddish-blue mark left by the tight vine. "Here, let me rub your ankle."

Toad held on to Miggy's shoulder and stretched out his chubby leg. She reached for the injured ankle, but now there was no mark on it at all. It had completely faded.

Amazing!

"Home," Toad said.

"Off we go!"

Miggy lifted him onto her shoulders and

climbed up the bank to the bridge. How happy she was that Toad had minded Pogg's rule about not crossing the logs by himself.

"Mogg will be so glad to hear about how you named the bunnies," Miggy told him.

She tried to act as if nothing bad had happened. Maybe her brother would get distracted and forget about it. Detouring off the path, Miggy set Toad down in a patch of pink larkspur. "Would you like to pick another pink flower for Mogg?"

That brought a smile to Toad's face. He picked a handful of pink blossoms.

Miggy lifted him back onto her shoulders. As she trudged along the path toward home, she thought about the magic that had happened both times she'd used the dragon stone. And one question kept troubling her mind:

Was it right to keep the stone's awesome power all to herself? The magic seemed far beyond anything that should belong only to her.

CHAPTER 13

THE FESTIVAL

Back at the cave, Miggy watched her mother fuss over the pink flowers Toad had brought her. He told Mogg all about the bunnies and made no mention of getting caught in the snare.

Miggy couldn't feel more relieved.

Mogg and Pogg were ready to leave for the festival, so off they all went. They carried bundles on their backs filled with wares they hoped to sell throughout the day.

Miggy held tight to Toad's hand as she followed her parents through the woods. Mogg, with a sprig of pink larkspur behind one ear, also carried a basket Miggy had helped her weave. The basket was filled with apples and walnuts.

Pogg carried a spear in one hand and a bone club in the other. Both were marked by a tiny leaf he carved on everything he crafted.

Carrying weapons today was a smart idea in case any wild animals picked up the delicious scent of roasting fish and decided to join the festival.

Soon, they stepped out of the woods and into Permian Park. The grassy meadow, shaded by a few ancient trees, was bursting with Clan members. Greetings filled the air:

"Hello, old friend!"

"How was your summer?"

"Good to have you back in Rocky Creek!"

Six fires warmed the air with fish roasting on spits above them. Kids of all ages raced through the crowd playing tag.

Miggy was eager to dash off and find Willow and Twig. But she had to wait until her mogg took Toad. Miggy wanted to keep an extra eye on him after what had happened at the creek.

Music filled the air. Miggy knew its source:

Old Tanner and Woolly. Any gathering was an excuse to play and sing and dance.

Animal skins dotted the grass. Arranged on top of them were food and crafts for sale. Miggy hoped Willow's mogg was here somewhere, selling bone necklaces.

Across the park, foot races had begun. The grannies usually stood by to tend to scraped knees and other injuries. Miggy glanced around, but the grannies were nowhere in sight. Maybe they hadn't arrived yet.

Mayor Magnon blew into an ox horn to silence the crowd. "Welcome," he began. "We are here to celebrate the end of summer and the return of the Clan to Rocky Creek."

The crowd hooted and cheered. Miggy joined in.

"Eat, eat!" the mayor hollered.

Miggy ate with her family—roasted fish with ginger root, roasted apples, and walnuts. And, for dessert, sweets made out of syrup from

Mrs. Sapien's trees. She was the best baker in the Clan.

After lunch, Miggy's mother took Toad to sit with her behind her display of baskets, rugs, jewelry, and blankets. Pogg's display of tools and weapons was nearby.

"Where are the grannies?" Miggy asked.

Her mother glanced around. "They'll be here soon. They always chant a blessing for the Clan at every festival."

Mogg turned her attention to a customer, so Miggy ran off to look for Twig and Willow. She found them helping Woolly sell some of his father's musical instruments.

Other kids from school joined them, sitting on the ground in a circle. They talked about the fun things they'd seen or done over the summer.

A girl named Breeze told about seeing a strange animal with polka dots on its fur.

"Wow," said Miggy.

An older boy, Hawk, talked about learning how to build a canoe and sail it across a lake as big as all of Rocky Creek.

Miggy got chills at the thought. "Wow."

The twins, River and Rain, told about seeing swirling winds of sand bounce and twirl across fields.

"Wow and wow!" said Miggy. That was the most amazing story of all.

The exciting tales made Miggy sigh as she thought about her own summer: Hunting for the right sized bones and stones. Reeds and seeds. And watching out for Toad.

Ho-hum.

Placing a hand over her belt pouch, Miggy gave the dragon stone three pats. *Here is my wish: Someday I want to tell a story that will make everyone* else *say, "Wow!"*

CHAPTER 14

BONE NECKLACES

The boys ran off to start a rock-throwing contest.

Miggy and Twig stayed behind to help Willow and her mogg lay out a jewelry display.

While they waited for the first customer, Willow's mogg gave the girls a lesson on how to make a bone necklace.

Twig strung three tiny bird bones on a thin beetle vine to make hers. Miggy strung fish bones with little white river shells in between.

When the necklaces were finished, the girls helped each other tie the ornaments around their necks. Miggy was thrilled to have her own bone necklace—but she was also distracted.

The whole time she'd been working, she watched for the grannies. What was taking them so long to get here? Did they need help carrying things?

ture was wedged between the walls
on.

ht.

v minutes, its enormous tail swished
orth, making the ground tremble
the tail smashed into the walls of
vs.

ight!

verruled her fear. She wondered if
half of the creature qualified as an
sighting.

rept closer, keeping a safe distance
rashing tail. She was glad the dino
ee her.

een the thunderous smashing, she
s.

nnies!

ldn't see them or hear what they
, but she felt sure they were well out
the *other* end of the Spin—the end
assive alligator jaws.

"Let's go find the grannies," she said to her
friends.

But Willow's mogg needed her to stay and
help sell jewelry. A line of eager customers had
formed. Twig offered to keep making necklaces
so the buyers would have lots of choices.

Miggy wandered to the edge of Permian
Park, but there was no sign of the grannies.

She glanced back at the festival. Clusters of
Clan members gathered here and there, mov-
ing among the displays to see what everyone
had brought to trade and sell.

Miggy sighed. All her friends were busy, but
she could go look for the grannies. It wasn't far
to their cave—just out of the park, through The
Narrows, and off toward Lizard Lake. Maybe
she would run into them before she got too far.

Miggy took off, swerving through the aspen grove that bordered the park. She walked
for the same amount of time it took to eat
two pears. Then she came to The Narrows, a

canyon formed by high red-rock walls on either side.

The air cooled as she entered The Narrows because the walls blocked the sun. Miggy followed the trail as it zigged and zagged through the canyon. Even the sand beneath her feet was red.

When she was at the halfway point, the ground began to tremble.

Uh-oh, she thought. Only one thing made the earth shudder like that.

Something gigantic.

Something heavy.

Something dangerous.

Like a Spin.

A STIC

Fear tingled up M citement.

A Spin! Would s

Suddenly, she re the canyon to hide run the lumbering

As Miggy bega exploded ahead of

Oh! The creat was up ahead. Be cave.

No wonder the g festival yet, she th *their way.*

Miggy rounded *There it is! A real,*

Or the backsid

The of the c

Stuc

Ever back ar each tir The Na

Wha

Thril seeing o actual S

Migg from the could no

In be heard vo

The g

She c were sayi of reach with the

The strange chitter-growl burst again from those jaws.

Miggy stood in awe as she studied the thin spine, rising like a giant leaf in the middle of the creature's back. She wished she could see all of the Spin, but it seemed quite stuck.

This must be the mama, she thought. *What is she doing so far from her nest? Looking for food?*

Miggy wondered why the grannies hadn't come up with a spell to free the Spin.

Wait.

If the grannies helped the Spin get unstuck, he might eat them for lunch instead of saying, "Thank you." As long as he couldn't move, they were safe.

But if I use the dragon stone, she reasoned, *maybe I can free the Spin* AND *keep the grannies safe at the same time.*

Miggy paced back and forth across the narrow passage. She had to choose her words carefully to make the magic work.

Taking a deep breath, she reached into her pouch and took hold of the cold dragon stone. Immediately, it warmed inside her hand.

"Set the Spin free," Miggy told the stone. "And make sure it does not see the grannies. Or *me,*" she added as a quick afterthought.

A sudden whirlwind whooshed through the canyon, blowing Miggy's hair over her eyes. Keeping one hand around the dragon stone, she brushed her hair back with the other hand so she could see what was happening.

Angry clouds spread across the sky so quickly, it looked as if they were racing each other. Shadows cast the day into darkness.

The Spin's tail froze in mid-swoosh. The creature rose up tall, then with a creak and a crack of boulders, the dino began to move forward.

Miggy wasn't sure whether the Spin shrank or the walls of The Narrows widened. Either way, Mama Spin was definitely unstuck.

The second part of Miggy's request made her

clasp the dragon stone even tighter and chant, "Pay no attention to the grannies. Pay no attention to the grannies."

As she watched, the Spin plodded straight ahead. It did not look left. It did not look right.

Now Miggy could see the grannies. She held her breath, watching the Spin move between the sisters as though they were not even there.

Miggy pulled her hand from the pouch and shook her fingers. They ached from grasping the stone so tightly.

"Why, look, there's Miggy!" called Fauna, the younger sister. Her wild hair was caught up on top of her head with combs made out of pinecones. And on both wrists, she wore brightly beaded cuffs.

Flora, the older sister, wore a dangling scarf which Miggy recognized as a river vine from the overhanging trees on the banks of Rocky Creek.

On her belt, Flora wore many pouches.

Miggy knew they contained items needed for various spells.

"Child, what are you doing here?" Flora asked. "You could have gotten hurt."

"You two could have gotten hurt as well," Miggy replied.

Flora nodded as she gave Fauna a stern look. "Thank the earth my sister's spell finally worked on that beast. I don't know why the magic took so long."

Fauna looked flustered. "It must have been the drag . . . uh, I mean, *you* know." Putting a hand over her lips, she glanced at Miggy.

Miggy knew exactly what Fauna had meant to say. *It must have been the dragon stone.* But Fauna could not mention her own dragon stone or its magic would no longer work for the sisters.

"You mean, it must have been the *cracked* 'you know'," Flora shot back as she flung the dangling vine over one shoulder.

"I'm sorry I dropped it and messed up its power."

"Well, at least it worked," Flora snipped. *"Finally."*

Fauna sighed. "Let's get on to the festival. We're late."

Miggy turned to follow the grannies back the way she'd come.

So. Fauna *had* been weaving a spell to free the Spin. But her spell failed because she'd used a damaged dragon stone.

Still, the grannies *believed* their magic had worked. And that's all that mattered right now.

As they wove through The Narrows, Miggy wished the grannies would walk faster. Her heart was still racing from the giant scare.

"I've never heard a Spin make that shrill sound before," Fauna said. "Have you, sister?"

"No," said Flora. "I wonder what it meant?"

Miggy couldn't believe what she was hearing. "You mean, you both have seen a Spin before? And heard one, too?"

"Why, yes, child," Flora said. "In our generation, Spins were more common. This is the first one in Rocky Creek since we were girls."

"Wow," Miggy said. Even the grannies had amazing stories to share. Maybe she should tell them about the nest of Spin eggs. But before she could say a word, the earth began to tremble. Again.

"Oh, no," Miggy said, hearing the fear in her own voice. "Is it coming back?"

A ferocious roar ripped the air. This one was many times louder than the mama Spin's shriek.

Rising in front of them, above the walls of The Narrows, appeared a Spin much larger than the one they'd just freed.

"Oh, bones!" cried Flora. "There's another one!"

"A *bigger* one!" Fauna added.

Miggy stared at the creature. It was magnificent.

And utterly frightening.

Of course there were two of them, she told herself. *After all, there was a nest. This must be Papa Spin.*

And the mama's shriek?

I'll bet it's their cry for help, Miggy thought. *Papa Spin was probably watching the nest when Mama Spin sent out a distress call.*

And now, Papa was blocking their exit from The Narrows.

An answering roar echoed through the canyon from Mama Spin, who was at the other exit.

Miggy hugged herself and shivered.

They were trapped!

CHAPTER 16

THE POWER OF THE STONE

Papa Spin dipped his long neck over the top of the canyon wall as if he wanted to get a better look at them.

Miggy and the grannies scuttled backward, out of reach of the gaping jaws with teeth the size of river rocks.

Sharply pointed river rocks.

"Try the spell again!" Flora hollered at her sister. "Quick!"

Miggy watched as Fauna frantically checked beneath the lamb's-wool cover of her spell basket to make sure the correct items for this particular spell were there. Then she lifted the basket toward the creature and chanted:

> *In the dark of night or early dawn,*
> *we say to this beast: Be gone! Be gone!*

Miggy held her breath.

try the spell with pinecones and rosebuds."

"No!" Fauna shouted back. "That will bring butterflies."

"Oh," said Flora. "Not a helpful solution." Closing the pouch, she laid one hand thoughtfully over the other. "How about filling the basket with honeybees?"

"That will make all the water in Rocky Creek dry up."

"Not good," Flora said.

A moment later, she furiously began picking up red pebbles from the path. "I know! We can lay out seven circles of rocks, and—"

"Sister, no! That will fill The Narrows with tigers."

"Oh, potatoes!" said Flora, dropping the pebbles. "The last thing we need right now is tigers."

As Papa Spin wiggled his way further into The Narrows, part of the wall collapsed.

Terrified, Miggy clutched her belt pouch

and dodged rocks as they rained around her. *Stop waiting for the grannies to think of another spell! None of them will work without my dragon stone.*

Why had she ever thought it was a good idea to keep the stone hidden at home beneath her sleeping mat? The Clan needed protection from these creatures that had decided to start a family in Rocky Creek.

Flora and Fauna will know how to cast a spell for protection. If I were to try, I could make a huge mistake, thought Miggy.

The worry made her untie her belt pouch and take hold of the dragon stone. The grannies were debating whether or not an army of mice might scare away the Spins. And, if so, how would they then get rid of the army of mice?

While the two were distracted, Miggy secretly lifted the lamb's wool cover on Fauna's basket. She plucked out the damaged dragon stone and replaced it with her own.

Then she tugged on Fauna's sleeve. "Please, can you try the spell one more time?"

"I've already cast it twice," Fauna told her.

Flora was watching Miggy with curiosity in her eyes. "But the child does have a point. It took three tries earlier before the spell worked."

The sudden creak and crack of breaking boulders made Miggy and the grannies flatten themselves against the far wall as the Spin's opened jaws came closer.

Fauna thrust the basket toward the creature and hollered:

> *In the dark of night or early dawn,*
> *we say AGAIN, you beasts: Be gone!*

As quick as a bee sting, quiet filled The Narrows.

The Spin's jaws snapped shut. He lifted his head and gave a sweet chortling sound, like a kitten's purr.

Mama Spin chortled an answer.

Drawing back at the same time, the Spins turned in the direction of Half-Moon Cliff and their nest of eggs. They lumbered off as if they'd just been out for an afternoon stroll.

"I've never seen a spell work so well on the third try!" Fauna said, looking quite pleased with herself.

Flora continued to eye Miggy. Did the granny suspect she had something to do with the spell?

"Can we go to the festival now?" Miggy asked, hoping to avoid questions.

The grannies laughed at such a normal question after the terror they'd just been through.

"Lead the way," Flora said.

"And here, carry the spell basket for me," Fauna added.

As Miggy took hold of the basket, her hand tingled as if the dragon stone was telling her it was still nearby, and that she'd absolutely done the right thing.

CHAPTER 17

THE GRANNIES' BLESSING

Mayor Magnum stepped onto a flat tree stump and blew into the ox horn a second time.

The crowd stopped to listen.

"It's tradition at our festival to have the grannies give the Clan a blessing for the coming winter."

Everyone stopped what they were doing and gathered by the fishpond.

"There you are," Twig exclaimed as she and Willow ran up to stand beside Miggy. "We couldn't find you for the longest time."

Miggy shrugged. "I went to find the grannies, then walked back with them."

"Oh," Twig said. She pretended to yawn at what sounded like a boring jaunt.

If she only knew, Miggy thought.

Flora greeted the crowd. "We shall recite a

chant over the spell basket. Then at dusk, we will bury it near the archway into Rocky Creek. This will protect our homeland and bring safety and happiness to our Clan."

The exact spot where the basket was buried changed every year. No one knew but the grannies.

Standing up tall, Miggy waited for the blessing. This was one of her favorite parts of the festival.

Fauna set the basket on the flat tree stump, raised both arms over it, and chanted:

> *Chicken bone, secret stone.*
> *Twig of pine, grapefruit rind.*
> *Cat's claw, Granny's shawl.*

Miggy noticed two things. One, a small piece cut out of Flora's shawl must have been sacrificed for the blessing.

And two, the chant did not reveal the dragon stone.

Fauna continued:

Abundant rain in our domain.
Streams of fishes, brimming dishes,
Clan of health, Clan of wealth.

Fauna paused, as if preparing one more chant, previously unplanned:

Protect our home from creatures' claws.
From pointed teeth and mighty jaws.

Relief washed over Miggy. The three blessings felt like warm blankets settling over every member of the Clan.

And now Rocky Creek would be safe from the Spins.

"Look!" called Stone from his perch in a monkey tree.

Everyone followed his gaze. The sun was breaking through the dark clouds.

The grannies always said if sunlight shone on the annual blessing, it was an omen that good luck and good hunting would be with the Clan for a year.

The crowd cheered as they went back to the festival activities.

"We're starting a game of Triassic Trivia in the aspen grove," Woolly called. Stone hopped out of the tree and followed his friends across the park, but Miggy hung back.

"Aren't you coming?" Stone called to her.

"In a bit," Miggy answered. She needed another moment alone with the grannies.

Fauna untied one of her beaded wrist cuffs. "This is for you," she said as she fastened it around Miggy's wrist.

"Go play with your friends now," Flora told her. "You deserve a little festival fun."

Miggy hugged the grannies and thanked them. Then she dashed off across the grass for a round of Triassic Trivia.

And she knew the exact question she would ask when her turn came:

"Who in the Clan has seen a Spinosaurus for the first time in two generations?"

No one would know the answer, except her: "Me, me, me!"

Miggy laughed out loud as she ran.

Finally, something exciting has happened to me. And, when I tell my story, everyone will say, "Wow!" because I wished for it on the dragon stone.